MW01132888

RANGER

THE LITTLE HORSE WITH THE BIG HEART

CHRISTY WOOD

ILLUSTRATED BY PAUL PARTON

To Carl,
Keep doing your best!
Christy Wood

authorHOUSE®

AuthorHouse™
1663 Liberty Drive
Bloomington, IN 47403
www.authorhouse.com
Phone: 1-800-839-8640

Published by AuthorHouse 10/19/2012

ISBN: 978-1-4772-6750-9 (sc)
ISBN: 978-1-4772-6749-3 (e)

Library of Congress Control Number: 2012916764

Any people depicted in stock imagery provided by Thinkstock are models, and such images are being used for illustrative purposes only. Certain stock imagery © Thinkstock.

This book is printed on acid-free paper.

Because of the dynamic nature of the Internet, any web addresses or links contained in this book may have changed since publication and may no longer be valid. The views expressed in this work are solely those of the author and do not necessarily reflect the views of the publisher, and the publisher hereby disclaims any responsibility for them.

DEDICATION

To all the wonderful horses God has created
May every human be blessed to have a horse like Ranger

TABLE OF CONTENTS

FOREWARD

A foal is born under difficult circumstances. He proves he is a cleaver survivor and grabs at the precious life that has been offered to him. A young women's husband buys this special horse for her and a deep attachment develops between equine and human. They live through many amazing and exciting adventures. He captured the hearts of everyone who knew him and these are just a few of the special people who remembered him:

I remember the first day I met Ranger like it was yesterday. I arrived at the Wood"N"Horse Training Stables to take my first horseback riding lesson ever! Ranger was tied to the hitching post, his ears forward, looking right at me. It was as if he was greeting me with a smile! The morning sun was shining on him and he was glowing like a brand new copper penny. I thought he was the most beautiful horse I'd ever seen. I learned to groom, saddle, clean feet and bridle that morning, while Ranger stood quietly. He was patient as I made mistakes and fumbled with the new tools I was learning to use. If horses could talk he would have been saying, "That's okay! I've got time, you'll get it." We had a wonderful ride that morning and many more after that day. Ranger gave me the first understanding of friendship and partnership with a horse and it's carried with me throughout my life with each and every horse I've known. Erin Farnsworth

My most vivid memory of Ranger speaks of his devotion and loyalty

to Christy. One afternoon, after giving a riding lesson, Christy let Ranger loose to graze the rich, green grass in the backyard while she finished up chores around the barn. But he, instead, chose to follow her around while she worked. That spoke volumes to me of his big heart and love for Christy.
Vicki Blakslee

Ranger was better than any horse you could hope to own. His soul was the presence of calm and comfort. His mind was an unassuming brilliance. His antics were memorably endearing, thus this book, and his heart captured everyone, especially mine. Thank you, my dear friend, Ranger, for the rides at your home, the beach, and Santa Barbara.
Lynn Meier

If I have learned anything about horses it is that regardless of breed, bloodlines, or color, a good horse is a good horse. You can't ride registration papers and that's a good thing, because Ranger didn't have any. We knew very little about his lineage. Ranger was to be a trail horse for me but turned out to be so much more than that. He wasn't just another horse in the barn, he became a member of our family. No matter what you asked of him, he came through for you. I have fond memories of our hunting trips together, rides on the beach and watching Christy pony young horses in the surf with him. Ranger lived to be your friend and to please. His attitude, disposition, and ground manners were unbeatable. His best attribute was his big heart. I feel truly blessed to have had him in my life. Steve Wood

RANGER

THE LITTLE HORSE WITH THE BIG HEART

BY

CHRISTY WOOD

MY BEGINNING

Mom must have been frightened. In her innermost being she must have known she was going to have a baby. But the rancher who owned her had no knowledge of the fact that a young yearling stud colt running with his horse herd had the moxy to be a sire. My mother, a chestnut mare, the color of a copper penny, was turned out on Wutchumna Mountain for the winter. I was going to be her first foal. As an expectant mother she tried extra hard to find grass and bark that would nourish the foal growing inside her.

As the time grew closer for my birth and arrival as one of God's precious creations on His earth, an arrival of a negative sort was brewing in the clouds. Tulare County was slated with a winter storm warning. The creeks were rising and the snow level dropping. Wutchumna Mountain was smack dab in the middle of the storm. The day started out dark and gloomy, cold and miserable, and this carried on into the dusk. Mom put her head down and turned her rump to the wind, as all horses do to survive the elements, and noticed the pains that were starting in her abdomen.

I was anxious to get out. My muscles had been twitching and contracting for months in preparation to make my legs strong enough to help me stand for the first time. I could feel the temperature rise around me and a tightening of Mom's muscles as she started to labor with my birth.

She was nervous. Down she would go to the ground, pushing, then up again walking in circles, sweating and panting, then down to push again. My instinct told me to get into a diving position with my head between my front legs to become more streamline and to make myself smaller to go through the birth canal. A few more pushes and grunts from Mom and I was suddenly in shock of how cold I was becoming. I felt the stretch of my front legs pierce the rubbery sack that surrounded me. I gasped for my first breath of air – I was alive in my mother's world. Mom, I'm here! I've arrived! I longed to touch noses with her and memorize her scent. As I tried to open my eyes, the freezing rain kept weighing them down. My body felt stuck in the mud and it took all of my strength just to sit up so my lungs could take in the air I craved. The winter elements of wind and rain were tapping the life from Mom and me. We were both weak. She raised her head from her prone position on the ground and welcomed me. I sensed her love. What a sweet whinny she had. She made a grand effort and stood up. She was bigger than life to me. I desired to stand beside her, but my legs would not cooperate. They were going in four different directions. If I got my front legs up, my backside was down. When my back legs pushed my rump off the ground, I could not get my nose out of the mud. I wanted to be a horse – I was going to be a horse – I told myself. Mom gave me a gentle nudge. You can do this, son. Okay Mom, this is for you. Oh my gosh, I'm standing. I wish the ground would stop moving. It's not the ground, Son, you just have to get your coordination and strength. She knew that once I stood then nourishment from her milk would be the next important task for me. She positioned herself next to me, facing the opposite direction and even turning her inside thigh to make it easier for me to tuck my head under her leg to reach her udder. But in disappointment for both of us, she had not developed any milk for me to drink. She kept nudging me to try in hopes that something would flow from her nipples.

As minutes and then hours passed, I started to feel despair. Hunger and weakness took its toll, and I collapsed to the ground. Would I have enough strength to get up again? Thoughts invaded my mind that I had more of a purpose than to live just a few hours. I felt an urgency to be the horse that God made me to be. To carry on for my ancestors. Historically, horses had gone on before me to carry great armies into battle, conquer kingdoms, and win the West. My Mom was the last vision I had as my eyes closed and my thoughts were stilled.

I slowly began to hear voices of the human kind. I saw shadows as my eyes opened to the morning light. The storm had passed. My mother's owner and another rancher stood over me and discussed my plight. What should we do with this half dead colt? I heard one man ask. It took all my strength, which wasn't much, to raise my head as I tried to show the two ranchers I was worth helping. Mom's owner suggested the neighboring ranch that recently had a family of four children move onto the hilltop property as a possibility. They may want to raise a colt as a family project. This sounded good to me. I would be cared for by four young'uns and have a family to grow up with. Both ranchers scooped me up in their arms and laid me in the back of a pickup truck on top of a saddle blanket. I glanced back to see my mother foraging on a large pile of hay the ranchers had brought for her. She was famished and ate quickly. I called to her as the truck slowly moved down the hill. Anxiety crept into my soul and we both knew this might be the last time we would see each other this side of Heaven. Mom ran to the edge of the pasture where the fence line kept her from following the truck. Mom, thanks for giving me life and trying so hard to care for me. I'll make it, I will live, and I'll make you proud. Her cries for me faded as we left the mountain on my way to the unknown for my future and my new home.

MY LIFE WITH HUMANS
AND OTHER HORSES

The road to my new home was long and windy. The truck went down from the mountain where I was born, through a canyon, then ascended the neighboring mountain range. As my head bounced in motion with the rough road, I was taking in how blue the sky was. It had a calming effect on me. I was at peace, even though I was hungry and now an orphan. Then a little house appeared on top of the hill. As the truck pulled into the yard, my new family, the Nelsons, emerged from their dwelling. The father was tall with a sense of authority. The mother had a sweet smile and kind eyes. The children, three girls and a boy, were all excited and rushed to me with cooing sounds. Their soft hands stroked my neck and I felt like I belonged here. As the ranchers lifted me from the truck bed, the hunger pains increased in my belly. They laid me in their garage on several soft blankets. To my relief, Mother Nelson approached me slowly with a bottle that had a chewy end and she inserted it into my mouth. I instinctively started sucking. Sweet, creamy milk flowed through the nipple and I knew this would give me strength and life. More, more, please! I drank until I was full and fell asleep content.

The first few days and weeks at the Nelson homestead were full of nourishment for my little body and the excitement of getting to know my new human family. I listened to the Nelsons trying to decide what name to give me. They sounded out everything from Apple to Zack. Then one of the girls spoke up and said, let's call him Wutchumna because that is the name of the mountain where he was born. Everyone seemed to like it, as did I. Good name for a war horse or a conquering equine, I thought. I was ready to conquer my world.

As my body grew, I learned how to become a horse. I could munch green grass and hay with my new teeth. I could outrun the family dogs in a game of tag. And I could jump any obstacle that got in my way. I found this out one day when I was running so fast I could not stop. So instead of crashing into a wheelbarrow, I just tucked my legs and propelled my body over it. That was exhilarating! I wanted to do that again. I watched my humans and saw how they opened gates, where they stored the dog food (one of my favorite treats), and memorized the sound of the family car as they drove down the mountain and went into town. I also knew the sound of the car returning as it climbed back up the hill and parked in the garage. This was especially important because when the family was gone, I had a secret playtime no human saw.

Most of my adventures took place when the Nelsons left their hilltop home for the day. When I heard their car engine fade into the distance, I would jump the pasture fence. The pasture bordered the family's backyard where Father Nelson meticulously mowed and watered his precious lawn. What a spectacular treat for me. The lush, thick grass became a regular part of my diet. I enjoyed snooping in the garage, too. When I first arrived on the Nelson ranch, before I was strong enough to stand up, I would look up from the comfort of my blankets and marvel at all the tools and paint cans. I was now big and smart enough to go exploring. I would use my nose to rearrange the tools. Paint cans tipped easily and left bright colors on the garage floor.

Now that I was strong enough to gallop around the hill top pasture, the Nelsons felt I was ready to meet the one other horse they had living on their ranch. His name was Roper. He was a 5 year old quarter horse gelding, large in bone and muscle with a deep red mane and tail that matched his body color. The Nelsons would tell people that Roper got his name because he was so hard to catch. A cowboy who trained him had to throw a rope over his head each time he went out to the corral to bring him in for training. Roper didn't like humans much, and only showed enough interest in them to get what he wanted which was food. He could be disagreeable at times, so he was only ridden by father Nelson. Roper wasn't a safe horse for young inexperienced riders.

I was happy to know there was another horse on the ranch and I was hoping Roper would be my friend. It would be fun to explore the hill top pasture and share adventures with him. I was lead up to the pasture fence that separated the two paddocks and was turned loose to meet my new friend. My instincts told me to lower my head with a sideways glance to show my submission and respect to an older horse. Roper walked towards the fence to meet me, but a few steps away from touching noses as all new horse friends do, he lunged at me with his ears pinned against his head and his teeth and mouth open to show anger. I quickly ducked away and he bit the fence right where I was standing. I was disappointed that one of my own kind would chase me away and reject any attempt from me to be my friend. I sought the comfort of my human caretakers instead. For a while, the daily grooming, pats, and treats were good enough for me. Eventually, the Nelsons turned me out permanently with Roper on the mountain pasture. I learned immediately to run and turn quickly to avoid Roper's bites and kicks. I gave him plenty of room when hay was put in our feeding tubs and I always let him east first. I was not going to let him discourage me from growing into the best horse I could be. I really have him to thank for making me try harder to be better and stronger than he was.

I wasn't old enough or tall enough yet to start the training to be a riding horse. The little Nelson girls wanted to start riding so the family bought a POA pony, which is an Appaloosa pony. He was a bright black and white leopard. His white hair was covered from head to tail with black spots. They named him DA, after Father Nelson's job as a district attorney. DA was short and very, very round. He wasn't as quick on his hooves as I was and so I felt the need to be his protector from Roper. I would block the mean lunges from Roper and gallop circles around DA, herding him away and out of danger.

DA and I had tons of fun together. I taught him how to open gates, as he was too fat to jump over the pasture fence. We discovered that the houseplants on the back patio were a tasty morsel before lunch. Then I shared my lush backyard grass with him, and we topped it off with doggie kibble from the garage. Soon, Father Nelson caught on to our exploits and padlocks showed up on all the gates and garage door. I still jumped my fences, but poor DA had no choice except to watch my antics from the pasture side of the fence. Roper was jealous of my ability to solve problems and the strength of character I showed towards my life with humans and other horses.

Then the day came that would forever change the direction of the rest of my life. The Nelsons called a local trainer who drove to the house on the hill a few times a week to start my education. I had heard them talk about this lady many times. She was a success as a world champion rider and trainer. I thought to myself that I could handle this big person and I wasn't going to make it easy for her. I was having too much fun each day to start going to horse training school. She showed up in the late morning that first training day. I did not expect what I saw next; the person who everyone described was bigger than life was indeed a petite woman. She was small like me and had a flaxen mane just like mine. Her name was Christy. Mother Nelson greeted her with a hug, a gesture humans did when they liked each other. She then walked with Christy over to my training corral. The instant we made eye contact with each other, our souls touched. A deep respect and connection was formed. Christy then made that same special gesture toward me and hugged my neck! I was hers forever.

Christy had a gentle touch and the understanding that a young horse needs time to learn at their own pace. This way I could absorb all of the training better. I was first tied to a hitching post with an inner tube to help me learn how to stand quietly without pulling back and hurting my neck. The inner tube would give way and then bring me back close to the post if I felt the urge to play while I was tied. Then I was sacked out with a plastic rain slicker. She took the slicker and rubbed it all over my body. Next a western saddle was introduced to my back. I carried a bit in my mouth as she taught me to lunge on a longline in a 30 foot circle. Here, I learned human verbal commands. They were walk, trot, canter and most importantly, whoa. Later when I was ridden, I did whoa so well, that it became a game for me to see if I could unseat the person who was sitting in the saddle when they asked for whoa. Christy always stuck to me like glue.

She then attached two long driving reins through the stirrups on the saddle and attached them to my snaffle bit. She stood directly behind me and lightly tapped the lines against my sides and asked me to walk forward. It was a strange sensation at first to have her behind me, as she had always stood to my side for lunging. She explained to me that this would change the direction of her voice so that it would be closer to where I would hear it when she was sitting on my back. Also, the lines touching me on my sides simulated how her legs would move as a light kick to move me forward. That is what was so special about my trainer. She would stand at my head, stroke my nose and neck, and talk to me with a soft tone and explain each day's lessons. Even though we spoke different languages, our spirits connected and we knew what the other was saying and, sometimes, even thinking. The next training step was Christy putting her foot in the stirrup, swinging her leg over my hip, and sitting softly in the saddle. She was so light. This being a riding horse was going to be easy. When she knew I was ready, she skipped all the preparation that day, and said,"Wutchumna, lets go. Walk out, buddy." And I did just that. We were a team, one unit, and partners for life. I was ready to be her war horse! The rest of my training days progressed quickly. I was trotting, cantering, spinning and, doing rollbacks and lead changes.

Father Nelson was so pleased with my progress that I soon found myself herding cattle that he had on his mountaintop ranch. He cared for me like I was another member of his family. My special friend and trainer, Christy, was coming to the Nelson ranch less frequently now. Her job as my trainer was done and she moved on to other horses. That last day I saw her reminded me of the last day I saw my mother. My heart was breaking for a second time. Christy felt it too, and she re-assured me that she would check up on me from time to time. I held onto that thought.

One spring day Christy showed up to help Father Nelson gather cattle. She rode DA and I carried Father Nelson over the rolling hills. My heart beat rapidly as I was very happy to see her again. I was also pleased that I was chosen by Father Nelson that day. I held my head high as I was lead from the pasture and I gave a cocky glance back at Roper who was left behind. My trainer and Father Nelson were having a friendly conversation as we rode through the colorful spring flowers on the hillsides. He was explaining to her about a career change he had accepted. He was going to move his family to the city. He explained that there would be no place for his family to keep DA, Roper and me. Fear started creeping into my heart. I did not want to go through the pain of losing another family. Being separated from my mother was hard enough for me. I was content with my life at the Nelson ranch. What would become of me? Father Nelson asked Christy to help him find a good home for DA and Roper. She said she would. Then I heard him say those chilling words – now about Wachumney? I hung my head and a tear started to form in the corner of my eye. I didn't like change, and yet, with each change in my life came another adventure and everything seemed to turned out okay. And then I heard those saving words. "Would you like to own Wutchmna," he asked? Within the time it takes to breathe in and use air to form a word, Christy said with enthusiasm, "Yes!" I wanted to squeal, run, and buck through the field of flowers to show my joy, but Christy's good training kept all four of my hooves firmly planted on the ground. I continued my responsibility for the human who was sitting on my back. Christy and I would celebrate later.

The last week the Nelsons spent at their hilltop haven was poignant for all of us. They had been so good to me. We had great times learning to be horse and horsemen. And, yet, I could not believe that I was going to go live with my special friend and trainer. Christy showed up with her matching truck and trailer, very fitting for this great war horse she was getting, I thought. I was already dreaming of the adventures that lay before us.

I soon discovered Christy had big plans for me, too. She gave many riding lessons at her ranch to beginning riders and thought that I had the ability to handle their inconsistencies. She also had a show team and was a horse show judge. I felt honored that she wanted me, even though I was not a fancy show horse. She talked about team sorting, penning cattle, and the mountain and beach rides she wanted to take me on. She was also a newlywed, and her husband, Steve, a firefighter, was just getting back into riding. She knew I would be a perfect mount for him, too. I proudly loaded into the trailer and left Wutchmna Mountain for the last time.

A NEW HOME

I never left the mountains my entire life. Christy's ranch was in the Sierra Nevada Mountain Range near the entrance to Sequoia National Park in California. The quaint little town where she lived was called Three Rivers. When we arrived at the ranch, I backed out of the two-horse trailer with wide eyes and my head up to take in my new surroundings. Wow, what a

neat place! There were several arenas; one had a full jump course set up and the other had an obstacle course complete with poles, gates, and a bridge. A hot walker and round corral were near two tack rooms. There were paddocks behind the dwelling where Christy and Steve lived that were shaded with tall sycamore trees and lined with grass like a park. Fruit-bearing mulberry trees were near each paddock, and I soon learned how sweet the berries and leaves were to eat. Christy would allow her taller horses to help her trim the overhanging branches when she led them by the trees. She did not leave me out. She would go get her branch clippers and cut some down for me. What a pal. Sweets from the sweet.

I was led across the road to a larger piece of property. There were wide, open spaces here. The hillside of six acres was crossed-fenced with three pastures, all shaded with oak trees. A larger pasture up front was reserved for me. How nice, I thought. I'll be even closer to my little lady when she comes to get me for our rides. There was a five-stall barn on this side of the road, too.

Christy led me into the pasture and took my halter off. Then she hugged my neck, kissed me on the cheek and said, " welcome to your new home, Wutchmna." I was so content just to stand there, that I didn't want to leave her side. She said this is all yours, buddy, go run and enjoy. She waved her arms and jumped up to start playing with me, so I joined in. Now it was my turn to celebrate. I kicked up my heels and ran laps around the pasture. Life was once again secure for me.

The next morning Christy and Steve walked up to my pasture and leaned on the gate. They watched me as I grazed on dew-drenched grass. I was also given some very tasty alfalfa hay. I heard them talking about a new name for me. Christy said she liked short, two-syllable names as it was easier for her in calling out the name of the horse during a riding lesson. They thought out loud and talked about me walking across the mountain range at my old home. Steve was a firefighter who was recently promoted to fire investigator and wore a gun to work everyday just like a forest ranger. Christy said, " That's it! We'll call him Ranger." My head immediately went up. I liked the sound of that name, too. I think I'll let them know. I ran to the gate. I breathed hot air on Christy's face as I tried to give her a wet horsey kiss." Look," Christy said, " he likes it, too." She stroked my head and nose. "Good boy, Ranger."

Later that day, Christy came and took me for a ride around the ranch. She tied a lead rope around my neck to the other side of my halter and then jumped on me bareback. She started giggling because she was thrilled that she could swing her leg over my back from the ground. She finally had a horse small enough to match her. She was five-foot-two and I was fourteen-one. A perfect match.

I met my other stable mates that day. One was Kyappo. He was Christy's show horse and a registered Appaloosa gelding. He stood 16 hands. Horses are measured by the hand, which is the width at the widest park of a man's hand and usually measures out to be four inches. He was very colorful, and I envied his spots. He was kind to me and we later shared

© PARTON

many rides together. Christy took him to shows and rode him on the trails in the mountains. Kyappo was a champion in the jumping arena and on the obstacle course. We shared stories at night about our fence jumping. He jumped inside the arena and won blue ribbons for Christy. I jumped out over fences to eat lush grass. I wonder who was the winner here? I think both of us were. The other stable mate was an older Appaloosa gelding called Tiger. He was good on the mountain trails and could carry a pack saddle. He was all white except for his red tail. I heard Christy talk about his blood lines and how he went back to some old foundation Appaloosa that was famous. Tiger didn't seem to care about that; he was only interested in how soon he would get more hay to eat. He gave me a kind greeting as well. It was nice and relaxing to finally have other horses accept me and welcome me to their herd. Life without Roper was going to be great!

Each morning Christy would come to feed hay to me and the other horses. She always had a little black dog with her that watched her do her chores. I heard her call the dog Turbo. She had short legs, pointed ears, and was very round. After Christy put an additional can of grain in my feeder, Turbo would come over and stand under the feeder. I guess I dropped a few morsels while I was chewing and Turbo was waiting there to scoop them up. We sniffed noses and became friends. When we were both done, Turbo would step back outside the fence line and bark at me. I am sure she was saying thanks.

Afternoons at the ranch were relaxing for me. I was usually done by noon with lessons, work-outs, or trail rides. As I was led back to my pasture to rest for a few hours, Christy would place a cover on my face that fit over my ears and eyes and closed around my jaw. It was comfortable to wear and gave me great relief from the flies that would bite and annoy my eyes and face. I could see through the face portion of the cover, so didn't have any trouble finding my way to my favorite shade tree for an afternoon nap. Christy called the cover a fly mask.

Late evenings were an adventure. After finishing my hay for the night, I would walk to a spot on top of one of the hills in my pasture, cock one hind leg, and wait for the night visitors to appear. They were mostly the four-legged kind. Deer came down out of the thick trees that covered the foothills behind my pasture to eat the new buds of baby fruit off the trees that surrounded the jumping arena. They knew no barriers as they jumped with ease all the fences surrounding the ranch pastures. Wild pigs, almost half my body size, would scramble under the fences and go straight for the lush green grass out in front of the big red barn. They snorted and squealed as they over turned the grass looking for worms and grubs. What a mess they left for Steve and Christy to clean up each morning. Also a furry animal, brown and grey with a bushy tail, would come out from under the haystack and try to steal some of my grain that dropped under my feeder. In the morning when my humans inspected the damage left behind by the night visitors, I would hear them say that the tracks left from the furry visitor belonged to a marmot.

I had a few winged visitors that claimed the tops of the tall trees in my pasture. They were very active after dusk. There were hoot owls, bats and turkey vultures. The owls would hunt mice and rats for food, and the bats scooped down on flying insects for their meal. The vultures would roost for the night, but never stopped squawking. I could also see a few snakes slithering by, but only on the borders of the fences as they were cautious of open ground where horses were walking.

Later in the year, the evenings brought a disturbing odor to the air. When I picked up the scent, I would turn my head in the direction of the stink and get a glimpse of a small, round animal, black with a white stripe down its back, waddling away from my area. I would give this little creature plenty of room and would find another spot to graze for the night. Several nights a week the hay and grain barn was attacked by the animals I called bandits. They had black masks on their faces and were not happy unless they were tearing open a sack of grain, popping the lids off of storage bins, or opening tack boxes. They used their paws like human hands and could climb the sides of the metal barn like a cat climbing a tree. Christy called them raccoons. It's no wonder I didn't get much sleep at night!

As my new year moved on at Christy's ranch, the seasons went through their change as well. Several hours after dusk one winter night, the sound of the winter rain drops on the metal roof of my barn stopped suddenly. It was silent. I stepped outside of my barn to see what was going on. Little flakes of moisture started to pile up on my neck and back. It started getting heavy, so I just shook it off. But as soon as I cleared my back, it was covered up again with these flakes of white. I ran to my stable mate, Kyappo, and showed him the new white blanket I had on my back. "Look I said. I now have Appaloosa color just like you! I hope this lasts until morning, so my special lady can see this."

As daylight came, so did the brightness of all the white around me. Everything on the ranch was covered in white. The jumps, the obstacle course, the truck and trailer, trees, fence posts, my barn, and me! I saw Christy come out of her dwelling and heard the excitement in her voice. I think this was something new for her, too. She was taking pictures of everything covered in white. She came over to my pasture and gave me a big grin. "Ranger," she said, "you became an Appaloosa over night." She talked to me and told me that these white flakes were called snow. She came into my pasture and moved the snow around on my back making impressions with her hand that made me look like I had spots. It was a fun morning to watch all the animals and humans on the ranch play in the snow. Little black Turbo had to leap just to get over the piles of snow, or rather inches of snow. She barked at me and turned circles so I started running small circles in my pasture too. Christy laughed and took pictures of her special dog and horse playing together.

My first year ended with Christy and Steve having their picture taken for their Christmas card sitting on Kyappo and me. I was truly a part of their family now. I wondered if they could see how happy I was and how grateful that I had such a wonderful place to live.

LESSONS AND WATER WINGS

At first, I was not sure I liked all the kids and new riders making mistakes on my back. I preferred a rider that knew what they were doing. Before I developed the patience that Christy taught me, I did have fun messing with those riders who just couldn't get the idea of riding. Oh, I didn't do anything really bad. I just took advantage when I knew it was the right moment. I had a few fun times, like the day Christy and a lady friend were riding in an open field that was covered in wild oats. We were going to canter through the oats on our way to some foothills, but I just couldn't resist the chance to stop and put my head down and graze for a few minutes. When I stopped, it was that great stop Christy taught me in my early years as a two-year-old. Of course, my unexpecting green rider came right out of the saddle and landed in front of my face. I also would deliberately dodge a few cues a rider would give me, just to see if they were paying attention to their lessons. Christy's riding students soon developed a pet name for my antics – the kids named me Roger Dodger. Then there were some very special people who came to the ranch for my help. Not every human or horse is born with full capabilities. When we sense that in our own species, we tend to protect and nurture those who need our assistance. Larry and Rick were two boys who needed to feel some self worth. Both boys were deaf. I took it easy with them and slowed my movements down to help them with their balance. Christy learned their language of signing, which was using her hands and fingers to make her verbal words come alive, and together we opened the wonderful world of horses to them. Patty was a girl with Down's syndrome. She understood every word spoken to her, but could only respond in her own language. She was fearful about being on my back and, yet, dearly wanted to be there. I let her think she was guiding me, even though I was making all the decisions. Her heart was happy after each hour we spent together. And then there was Roy. He was an older man with multiple sclerosis. Once he was a vibrant rancher and cowboy. He felt the need to push his body into remembering what it was like to sit on the back of a horse. My little size gave him hope that he could once again sit in the saddle. It took time and patience for Christy and Roy to get his legs over my back. I knew that I must stand still for this procedure to work. Did they know that the blessing was in the gift? To hear the jubilation in Roy's voice made me realize that I was fulfilling my purpose. I was helping these special people conquer their difficult world. I felt very proud knowing that faith and confidence was expected of me, and this war horse delivered! Together we conquered their special needs.

I greeted each new dawn with the anticipation of what I would learn today. Sure I was a well trained broke horse, but the horse life Christy and

Steve had in mind for me needed continuing education. Today it would be water training. I thought, this will be easy. I conquered water at my birth. I got myself up and out of the mud. As I found out early on, my experienced

trainer did not always take the easy road. She was an explorer. Sometimes I thought the tasks she was asking me to do would be impossible, but my trust in her always brought me through. She never put me in danger. When the tasks were complete, this little horse was standing tall. There wasn't anything that Christy and I couldn't do together.

So off to the river we went. That looks like a whole lot more water than what I was lying in on my birthday. And it's moving all the time. I stopped to take a look, sniffed the water, touched it with my nose, then put one hoof in, all with Christy's approval, of course. As I walked in a little farther, I enjoyed the sensation of the water moving around my legs. The cool water

was a welcome relief from the hot summer day. My little lady was full of praise for my acceptance of the water this day. The swimming hole we went to had a large boulder down at the deep end. Christy would swim her more experienced horses around the boulder. She told me that we would save that adventure until another day. A few days later, on our way to the river, I sensed an excitement in Christy's movements. When she rode me bareback on water days, I could feel her balance and leg cues more strongly. "Okay, Ranger, today we swim around the boulder," she said. "Are you ready?" Anything you want, boss, was my attitude as we entered the river. I became buoyant as soon as I left the shallow bank and moved to the center of the river. My tail streamed behind me like a rudder. I kept my upper lip pressed in toward my nostril to close off my air passage so water wouldn't go up my nose. I found it natural to paddle, and swimming became fun. Christy's light weight barely kept her on my back as I parted the water with my chest, so she hung on tight to my long, flaxen mane. Around the boulder I went, swimming with ease. I became such a good swimmer that Christy used me as a pony horse to help her lead her weanlings in the water for their first time. Old and young horses that Christy was training didn't hesitate once they saw my confidence in getting wet. Christy was also able to trust me with the precious cargo of youth riders and beginners on their first trip to the river. I even had a young boy from New Zealand swim me around the big boulder at the deep end. The river was a tranquil place for me, a place to soak and reflect on my wonderful life.

SAND, SURF, AND BABIES

I remember well my first trip to the beach. It was with Steve. He and Christy rode with friends who were in a Christian cowboy riding group. Christy was out of town judging a horse show on the weekend Steve and I went. It was a camp-out that lasted several days. There were individual corrals for each horse and plenty of room for human tents. The site was at the bottom of a canyon surrounded by eucalyptus-covered mountains. The ground was sandy and it made for a soft place for me to lie down. Each night the people would cook over an open fire and sing songs. They worshiped a great creator they called God. I had heard Christy and Steve talk about this person before. I wondered if He was the same God I was grateful to for giving me my wonderful life.

The aroma of hot coffee, bacon, and eggs stirred the camp in the morning. Steve fed me before he ate his own breakfast. I finished my hay by the time Steve came to saddle me up. The walk to the beach was hard work through the thick sand, but along the way there were sage bushes, sand flowers, and an occasional deer at which to look. Then I heard a thunderous roar. It got louder and louder as we approached the big, blue water. This water was enormous compared to the river at home. As we made it down the steep sand dune to the beach, I stopped for a minute. Steve let me look at the sea gulls, seaweed, and white-capped waves. We approached the edge of the water very slowly. I was unsure if the white foam creeping up to my hoof was going to sting or be hot or cold. When the foam got closer to my hoof, it made a fizzling sound and dissolved away. That wasn't so bad, I thought. As the tide rolled back to the ocean, it drew me in. I followed it until it started coming toward me again. The waves got larger and surrounded me, but the rolling motion soothed my tension. I had the ocean up to my belly. Steve and I had a super time running through the surf. On the ride back to camp, we stopped at a most unusual tree. It was a eucalyptus that had limbs twisted and turning, giving it the look of an octopus. Steve and the other riders thought it had been hit by lightning at one time, which caused it to split and spread. He rode me to the center of the massive tree and there we had our picture taken. That photograph was a topic of conversation at the ranch for years to come.

Christy started buying, training, and selling a few extra horses. She was a good trainer and an excellent judge of horse flesh. I can testify to that! She also kept a few broodmares in foal to raise babies. I liked the little ones. I felt very special being able to pony the baby horses down the road in traffic, through the streams and rivers, up mountain trails over rocks, and through cattle herds. It was a big responsibility. Two foals come to mind when I think back on all the weanlings and yearlings I ponyed; one good one and one difficult one.

A little filly was born whose mother was a racing quarter horse mare and the father an Appaloosa stallion. Her mom was gray and the father sorrel with a white blanket. The filly was solid brown except for a large white blaze that went from eye to eye. She looked like she had been hit in the face with a cream pie. And that is exactly how she got her stable name, Pie. She didn't stay brown for very long. By the time she was a yearling, she was pure white. She also grew like a well-watered weed. During her yearling year she passed me in height. It was funny one day when Christy and I were taking Pie for a trail ride, a passing motorist stopped his car and asked Christy why she wasn't riding the big horse. Christy answered, "Because she is just a baby." Later that summer, all the ranch horses and I got to go to the beach campsite again. This time I was in charge of getting Pie into the ocean. She was a sweet filly and very agreeable to everything I showed her. She had the same reaction that I did upon seeing the big, blue water for the first time. So Christy and I paused to let her look, then slowly progressed toward the foam and waves. I will always remember how Pretty Pie's face looked with her dark, black-lined eyes as wide as they could go, peering into the surf. She leaned into me and I reassured her that the saltwater would be okay. She calmly stepped in. Good girl, Pie! We galloped and played for hours in the surf. We traveled many miles that day, up and down sand dunes. I especially liked dunes because I would sink my hind end in the sand up to my tail and just float downhill with the drifting sand.

A few days later, as the sun was setting and the moon rising, I heard

© PARTON

the riders talking about a moonlight ride. I got all excited. I was hoping Christy would ask me to lead. Not all the horses and riders chose to go, but I got my wish. The moon was very bright and the sand so white that it seemed like mid-day. One of the horses that joined us was a palomino. His golden color reflected the moon-light so he was like a beacon for us all. We long-trotted through the sandy trails of sagebrush and frolicked like foals at play. The sounds of laughter from our humans were like a sugar-cube treat: sweet!

A beautiful black and white Appaloosa colt was born several years later. His stable name was Mickey, as he had a clump of spots grouped on his hip in the shape of Mickey Mouse. His mom was an ex-race horse that Christy had bought off the track and re-trained to go on and become a world-champion English horse in the show arena. Her name was Smoke

and she had a gentle and kind spirit. She had several foals, all the result of artificial insemination. I learned that this meant that the daddy horses did not have to be on our ranch at the same time as the mother horses. Because of this, Christy never got to know the stallions' personalities. Even though this colt was trainable by my top trainer's methods, he constantly tested his handlers and stable mates. When I would pony him for his lessons out of the arena, he would always try to bite me. By now

Christy had confidence in the manner with which I taught the babies respect on the trail. If they got forward of my shoulder, I would give them a little nip to let them know where the invisible line was that they should not cross. Mickey didn't take my nip as a lesson, but considered it a game I really earned my oats and carrots each time we took him out.

Summer was in full swing and the big trailer was packed with camping equipment, ready for another beach trip. I was already smelling the camp-fire and the salty ocean air and dreaming of my sandy corral when Christy came to console me for the job that lay before me. She needed to take Mickey to the beach to round out his training. Darn! She promised me that I would have my very own ride with her without leading a baby on next year's trip, but this was important for Mickey. Christy constantly had to challenge him to keep his attention as he was a fast learner. When we arrived at the camp site and got ready for our first ride of the day to the beach, I noticed she placed a saddle on Mickey's back. He was another large yearling in height and muscle, and he could handle the weight of a saddle. Then on went saddle bags. Good for you, Christy, I thought. If Mickey thinks he is an adult horse, then he should be treated like one. I knew the trail to the beach by heart. Christy could drape my reins around the saddle horn and ride hands free if she wanted to. We were on our way to take Mickey to the big blue water. He was so busy trying to get me to play with him that he didn't pay attention to where he was going. When we came down to the beach, Mickey stopped suddenly. The crashing waves caught him off guard. He may have had more body mass in his favor, but not enough experience, like I had, on how to deal with a juvenile mind. I tugged sideways throwing him off balance and he had to step forward to keep from falling over. Don't underestimate this war horse, young man, I thought. You're dealing with a pro here. Mickey was now standing in the surf. The look on his face was so different from my Pretty Pie. He was disgruntled and showed it by splitting his ears sideways and down. Pure defeat was on his face. I may be small, but I am mighty. This little horse conquered once again, I thought.

That was a turning point for Mickey. He accepted his lessons more readily and actually went on to become a national champion show horse.

He moved to a northern state near the Canadian border where his town got snow drifts of twenty feet. I wonder how he handled that challenge. By the way, Pretty Pie went onto become a multiple national, world, and supreme champion. I felt I played a part in both of their successes.

VACATION AND FUN

Life was busy at the ranch. Christy gave riding lessons to beginners, intermediate, and advanced riders. There were English and western disciplines taught that included jumping, trail, and reining. I helped with all of this. I could take anyone over a course of jumps and work a trail obstacle course without any faults. I was real good on flying lead changes, spins, and circles. Christy spent a lot of hours preparing her show-team members who competed in California, neighboring states, and world show competitions. I gave many of those members their start, but all of them later purchased registered horses they could show.

Christy was also a horse show judge with multiple breeds. I knew I was nothing special on the outside, not the prettiest horse to look at. My confirmation wasn't perfect, I was small, and didn't have the face of a movie star horse. But conquering horses do so with their spirit, and Christy loved me for what was inside, not out. She judged me with her heart, not her expert judge's eye. We were each other's champions.

Christy's judging duties meant she traveled most weekends around the United States and internationally. One day she came to get me as she had arranged a vacation spot for me. She would be gone for three weeks in Australia to judge. A neighbor had an unused pasture where the grass had grown knee-high. They had lost their horse six months ago due to old age. I remember the horse. She was a black mare with four white socks and a blaze. I never saw her ridden and she was always alone. She was happy when we rode by on our way out to the trails. She would run to the fence-line and squeal and strike with a front hoof. I greeted her with perky ears and a shake of the head. Christy thought it would be a treat for me to munch on all the tall grass in the now empty pasture. She rode me down the street to the pasture the day before she had to leave for overseas. I was led into the wind swept, long, tall grass, had my bridle removed, got that great hug around my neck from my little gal, and watched her close the gate. You would think my mouth might have been full of grass in just seconds, but I couldn't take my eyes off my petite owner. She blew me a kiss and said she would be back to get me in three weeks. I started to feel anxious again, that sinking feeling of being away from everything I knew and loved. If I could not see my human coming out of her dwelling each morning, then at least I wanted to be in my home pasture. As she walked out of sight, I started scheming on how I could get out of this pasture. A horse's dream of a lush pasture was my nightmare. I felt lost and forlorn, and I wasn't going to stay another minute behind this strange fence. I ran one circle around the pasture to pick up speed, then launched myself over the four foot, barbed-wire fence, clearing it with ease. That's what I do, conquer obstacles that get in my way. I galloped back - toward home and caught up with Christy just as she was turning into the ranch driveway. She turned to see why she was hearing the sound of horse hooves on the road and was pleasantly surprised to see me. "Oh my Ranger," she said with a choke in her voice." You just couldn't live without me." At that moment she realized the true devotion I had for her.

The spring progressed, and Christy and I started spending some much needed R & R together. It was nice to have a break from the lesson kids, and my special human needed time for herself away from life's pressures. She took me to a local play day one Saturday and we entered some fun game classes. They offered an egg-and-spoon race, and a dollar bill race, to name a few. I had a very smooth jog and lope, so it was easy for my human to balance on my back. It was a good feeling to hear Christy laugh, and I really liked all the praise she was giving me. Then we came to the premier event of the day: the boot race. All the riders had to take off their boots, mount their horses, and line up behind a starting line. When the signal to start was called, we had to gallop to the other end of the arena, where all the boots were stacked in a huge pile. The riders then had to dismount, find their boots, put them on, remount their horse, and run as fast as they could back to the starting line. This small chestnut horse and his petite blonde lady were undefeated champions in this event. Christy was quick, and I was quicker. It was interesting to observe such a competitive person as my owner still trying to win even in fun horse games. But conquerors are successful in all that they do, and they need a special war horse to take them there. The blue ribbon from the boot race was placed on my paddock gate that night. Christy wanted everyone to recognize her other champion that day – me!

We also started attending team pennings. I was good at traveling over mountains and foothills to gather cattle, so the penning became very natural for me. These events were held once a week at night during the summer months. I had to load up in my trailer and be driven 45 minutes to the arena. I watched for a while ring-side to see just what was expected

of me. Christy was always good at giving me time to observe new things. Three horses on a team had to cut out a certain number cattle, then drive them to the other end of the arena and push them into a small pen. Then a buzzer would sound and the people would cheer the team with the fastest time. I was best at going in the herd. I was not much bigger that some of those cows, but I was definitely smarter. Christy said I had "cow sense" because I could read and control a cow's movements. Can you guess how this turned out for us? Christy won money almost every time we showed up to team-penning. Being little seemed to have its advantage more times that not.

One particular night as Christy started my warm up of loping circles around the cattle arena, I heard a familiar whinny that made me think of my past. It was Roper. His new owner was riding him at a few sortings around the county. I always tried my best when Christy rode me into the herd, but today, even more so, I wanted us to win in a big way. I was hoping Roper would see how good my life had turned out. As we were teamed up for the evening, our first run was good, but Roper's team beat us by a few seconds. That was a practice run. The second run was for money and the win. Roper gave me a glance of pure contempt as though to say, "you puney little horse, you will never beat me." As I watched and waited for my second go, Roper's team went in next and one of Roper's team mates let a cow slip by the gate and their team received a no time. As our team entered the arena next and I walked slowly towards the center of the herd, moving my head from side to side, then I pawed the ground once to send the cows a message that I was in control. I got all three cows cut from the herd quickly and our team worked well together. We placed in the money on that run and beat Roper's team. As Christy rode me back to the trailer to unsaddle me, I saw Roper tied to his horse trailer. He knew he had been beat by the little horse with a big heart and he bobbed his head to say "you did good, kid." I never saw him again after that day. When the event was over, people came up to Christy as she was brushing me down and wanted to know more about her little horse. What are his blood lines, who was his trainer, and did you pay a lot of money for him were the questions they were asking. Christy said to the people that sometimes blessings come in small packages and that the finest planned breeding, and money spent on top trainers will never make up for what is in a horses heart. I agreed as I had conquered once again and was a champion war horse in the cattle arena for my little lady that day.

HUNTING TRIPS

Fall was in the air as I sensed a change in the weather with the nights getting cooler and the winds bringing more clouds to the sky. I was shedding the short hairs of my summer coat. It was time for Steve's annual hunting trip and I had good thoughts of carrying my human into the woods and forests of the big mountains. I liked the ride in. The trees were bigger and taller than the ones around the ranch, and little seedlings were sprouting up all along the trail. Pine cones covered the ground and chipmunk's scampered across the moss covered rocks. It was soothing to my ears to hear the wind blow through the pine trees creating a musical symphony of its own. It was an eight hour ride in to the camp. I was leading one of the other ranch horses, Tiger, as the pack horse who carried the food for the men. He did well to keep up with my stride as I walked down the trail. When we arrived in camp, Steve unsaddled me and removed the pack boxes from Tiger. He led us over to a nearby stream to refresh ourselves with cool water. That night Tiger and I stayed on a high line, a rope that is suspended above the ground that is tied between two trees. It gave us freedom to move around and nibble at some grass. The lead ropes attached to our halters were tied to the high line and were just long enough that I could lye down to sleep.

Steve had four men he always rode with into the backcountry. One man in particular stood out in my mind as he had an unpleasant nature. If he had been one of my herd when I was growing up, I would have stayed clear of him; A troublemaker of the worst kind. I tried not to get in his way, and I always hoped Steve would not hand him my rein or lead rope. His name was Dan. On one of the hunting trips he brought a young mare who had just been pulled away from her nursing foal. The poor mare was sad, nervous, and in discomfort because her milk sack was hard and swollen from lack of relief from her nursing foal. I tried to comfort her through the whole trip. The long ride into the base camp was hard on human and horse. The mare did not do well. The next day when all the hunters were leaving camp, Dan asked Steve if he could borrow me for the day. UGH! Steve said yes. Steve wanted to hunt his favorite ridge that was better traveled on foot, and he was a little sore from the ride in the day before. Dan was a tall man, thin, and rough in appearance. He was rough in his soul, too. But it was my responsibility to take care of the human sitting on my back. Dan put his saddle on me and off we went to look for deer. As the afternoon faded into dusk, I tried to urge Dan to turn around and make our way back to camp. I moved my head from side to side and then would look back. He didn't understand me. He was disgruntled that he had not seen a deer all day. He took it out on me with sharp tugs on my bit and swift kicks on my sides. I can't get him back to camp fast enough, I thought. He traveled with a flask that had a strong drink in it that changed his personality. And not for the better. With every drink, he got a little more sleepy and disagreeable. We finally turned around. When we did, Dan put his hands in his pockets, wrapped my reins around the saddle horn, gave me a hard kick, and told me just to follow the trail back to camp. I knew he fell asleep rather quickly as I could feel him swaying on my back. I had to work extra hard on my walk down the trail to keep him balanced so he would not topple off. Just before dark, I came to a fallen tree that lay across the trail. I stopped for a moment to size up the situation. The tree was rather long and had limbs spread out in all directions. The shortest and most efficient way for me to proceed would be to step over at the middle. But the large trunk of the tree was just too big for my short legs to take a step. I knew my ability as a jumper, remembering the Nelsons' place, Christy's jumping arena, and the neighbor's pasture. Getting over the tree would be a breeze. I leaned back on my haunches and sprung lightly over to the other side. That was easy, I thought, until I saw Dan hit the ground. He woke up instantly using angry words. I had never heard such language and tone in all my days. I don't think he was very happy with me. He got up, brushed himself off, and remounted. Oh great, I've done it now. This is the side of Dan I didn't want to see. Luckily, we were close enough to camp that his anger didn't last very long. As I carried him back into camp, grumbling and cursing, he rode me right up to Steve, dismounted, and threw my rein in Steve's face. He said, "You tell Christy to stop training every damn horse she owns to jump". Steve took care of me that night with a good grooming and some oats. I heard Dan talking around the campfire later that night that he would never ride me again. Good, I thought. It all worked out in my favor.

The next morning, Steve got up to turn me, Tiger, and the other horses out into the meadow to graze on bunchgrass. It tasted sweet and moist from the morning dew. I nibbled for a few minutes but found the majestic mountains just to tempting to only look at, so I gave Tiger a nod and we took off at a run to go explore more of the high country. Our hooves were beating the ground so hard with our vigorous romp into the mountains, that if Steve was calling to me, I never would have heard him. I knew he would be OK as he had all the pack boxes with him. Tiger followed me as I lead the way up the mountains. The other horses that Steve's friends rode into the camp stayed in the meadow. We had fun dodging tree limbs and fallen logs. I also jumped a few along the way too. We had made it to the top of the mountain crest and were rewarded by finding a hill top meadow. The grass was tall with the tops of each steam bursting open with seeds. Yum!

I lost track of time, but the sun did go down and rise up again bringing its warmth to the new day. As the afternoon approached, I heard a faint call, and it sounded like someone was calling my name. Oops, I forgot about Steve. I turned to track the direction of the voice and nudged Tiger to follow me. I went in search of the voice. Sure enough, it was Steve, on foot, of course, with a bridle and halter in his hand calling for me. There was a bit of stress in his voice, so I trotted up to him to greet him for his efforts on finding us. His body language softened and he said, "Ranger, you shouldn't have taken off running like that from camp. I thought you would be tired from your ride into camp and your ordeal with Dan. I hope you enjoyed your freedom because now you will be kept on the high line the entire trip. I lost a whole days hunting just looking for you and Tiger.

But I had instructions from Christy who told me to take care of you and bring you home safely. I need to keep my promise to her." So Steve jumped on me bareback, after putting the halter on Tiger, and we rode back to camp together.

The next morning things had changed. Steve approached me running his hands down my front legs, and slowly he buckled leather straps around my fetlocks. He called them hobbles. He told the other humans he needed to keep me closer to camp and that he could not risk me wandering off again. As the hunters ate their morning meal around the camp-fire, one by one they stood in amazement and told Steve to watch his horse. The hobbles were intended to restrict my walking steps but no one said I could not canter in slow motion to the next spot I wanted to graze. I just picked up both of my front hooves and put them down in perfect unison to enable me to move about the meadow. The hobbles did slow me down enough that I did not lose sight of camp again. Even Dan was amazed at how smart I was in learning so quickly to move about with the hobbles tied to my fetlocks.

Toward the end of the week, Steve rode me up to another of his favorite spots, Alpine Lake. He finally got the deer he wanted. It was a large-bodied animal with a big antler rack. Steve struggled with getting it on my back and it nearly filled up the front of the saddle. There was just enough room for Steve to get his leg in the stirrup and find room to sit behind the deer. Nightime fell and so did the temperature. It had gotten so dark that Steve could not see his hand in front of his face. He was worried he would not be able to find the trail. In much the similar way that Dan had given me my own rein to find my way, Steve made the same gesture. He wrapped my reins around the saddle horn with some slack and told me to find my way back to camp. He pulled his jacket collar up around his neck, put his hands in his pockets, and said, "Ranger, I am trusting you to get us safely to camp." There were clouds in the sky that blocked the shining stars and moon that would have guided me. What would a war horse do in this situation? I had to rely on my other horse senses. My hearing, sense of smell, and the built-in compass in my head all directed me. After many hours, I came to a sudden standstill. I thought I heard a faint whinny. It was my friend, Tiger. He was sending me a signal, and I quickened my pace as I answered his call. My whinny awakened Steve. He was so grateful to me for getting him back to camp. He told me, "good thing you got us back, Ranger, because Christy gave me explicit instructions not to return home unless I had you with me!" I enjoyed the reward of extra pats on the neck, oats, and the bragging rights from the stories Steve would tell in the future.

A FATHER'S LAST RIDE
AND THE PARK

I loved the people that belonged to me or, should I say, that owned me. Either way, life was good. I enjoyed teaching the littlest of kids not to fear horseback-riding. Many of those kids grew up to be champion riders. Christy always found creative ways to teach them. The first-time adult riders were challenging, too. One lady came to learn how to ride so she could take a pack trip in the mountains. She was seventy-five. My oldest rider was 82. It was Christy's dad, Lou. He rode a little over the years when family would come to visit in the fall for the holidays. I have him to thank for helping Christy become the equestrian she is today. She showed me a stick horse he made for her when she was two years old. It's obvious to me he also taught her honesty when dealing with people and the management skills to run the ranch. He also taught her the value of a dollar. I never went without the best hay and oats.

I had the honor and privilege to take Lou out for his last ride on horseback. There was a local radio station that had just installed a new antenna on a mountaintop behind the ranch. Lou was interested in radios, so Christy offered to take him up the mountain to locate the antenna. The trail was an old pack station trail that was steep and windy. We took it slow; after all, I was carrying precious cargo. Each year after the spring rain, the trail would be overgrown with new shoots from trees and bushes. Christy rode ahead to lead us up the trail and cut branches to clear the way. She would stop Tiger on narrow portions of the trail, dismount on his off side, and other times, while mounted, lean completely over to one side with only one foot in the saddle, just to get under the low branches she needed to cut. I made sure I stayed quiet, still, and balanced to keep her dad safe. The foothills were painted with a bright variety of colors from the wild-flowers like bush lupine, fiddle-neck, and popcorn flower, as well as the sweet fragrance from sage and manzanita blossoms. We took frequent rest stops mainly for Lou's sake, but I was always ready to push on. We found the antenna and Lou seemed to enjoy the discovery. We stayed on top of the mountain for quite awhile, taking in the view. We lived in a canyon with several rivers running through. The nearby mountains had a waterfall and snow-capped tops. It is truly God's country. Christy and her dad had a special time together that day. A few years later, a foal was born on Lou's birthday, and Christy called him Louie.

Christy was continually looking for new places to trail ride. Her adventurous nature took her to Sequoia National Park to explore Redwood Canyon and Weaver Lake. These locations are an easy drive from the ranch as the Park's southern entrance is only six miles away. The trails are higher in the mountains, so we only had a few months in which to ride without bad weather - from July to September. On one late August ride, a cold front had come in early. On this ride were Pie and her owner, Erin, one of the kids I originally taught to ride, and of course, my beloved Christy. The ride to Weaver Lake starts by crossing a stream with a large water hole. All the horses I have ever led up there balk at this water hole. They just need a confident leader and I'm the horse for the job! This day, however, the water hole was covered with ice. Pie put on the brakes and did not want to go first. I don't think she had ever seen ice on top of water before. She lived in a warm stall during the winter months in the big red barn at the ranch and had not experienced living out in the elements. I, on the other hand, knew how to break water with my chin when the top of my water trough was frozen in the winter. I went forward slowly and put my hoof at the pond's edge. The ice cracked. Then an air bubble moved along under the surface looking for an escape. I found that fascinating. I also liked the crackling sound as I moved across the frozen water. I blazed a trail for my Pretty Pie. Christy and Erin both like to gallop, so up the trail we went through the redwood trees. The girls laughed, Pie squealed as she went first, while I followed with her pretty, long, white tail flowing in my face. We had a wonderful ride.

THE RESCUE

There can be a harmony and rhythm between horse and human. If we respect and listen to a human asking us to do something through their "aids," our union will be perfect. The human aids are voice, seat, hands, and leg pressure. A horse's reaction can be compliance or resistance. Many humans struggle with this concept and need lessons or training in the proper way to communicate with us. If this is not properly learned, horse and human become frustrated and confused. That is exactly what happened to one horse and rider during one of Christy's camping trips to the beach.

The day started out uneasy when tense voices filled the morning air. Jim and his wife were having a disagreement about something. The other riders stayed out of his way, finished their breakfast, and started to saddle up. After Jim haltered his horse and tied him to his trailer, I heard the turmoil continue. His horse would not stand still and instead paced back and forth, stirring up a lot of dust. His horse was not happy about his owner being so uptight. Jim's voice got louder and I could hear his frustration. I got the impression he was not experienced when it came to communicating with a horse. Everyone was saddled and ready to leave camp. Jim was the last one to be mounted. I noticed he was wearing a helmet, the only adult doing so. It would turn out to be a life-saving choice for him. We made our way to the beach on my favorite trail of sagebrush and sand dunes. My special lady was riding me this day and we led the procession. I could not have been happier. Jim left camp in the middle of the riders, but his horse gave him trouble most of the way to the beach. His horse spooked at everything and nothing. When we reached the ocean, Christy and I made our way into the surf. I was drawn to it like a magnet. I also liked the "atta boy" Christy gave me each time we jumped a wave. We played for a while chasing sea gulls and having mock races. I couldn't beat some of those long-legged horses. My heart was big enough, but my legs were just to short.

©PARTON

All too soon, it was time to head back to camp. We took a ridge trail that followed along-side a canyon, then ascended a mountain-side to some tall trees on the top. We started down one side of the canyon and came upon a small stream. Most of the horses followed my lead and walked over the water at the middle, but not Jim's horse. The humans were saying his horse decided he didn't want to get his hooves wet. But I knew it was an issue of trust. The frightened horse lunged sideways, taking Jim through the bushes that were mostly in poison oak. That ugly human language began that made me so fearful and uneasy. Christy sensed my tension and with the stroke of her hand, reassured and calmed my spirit. As the trail began to climb, I led the way. The route was narrow with many twists and turns. Suddenly, I heard the sounds at the back of the group that worried me. It sounded like the quick steps that a horse takes in hopes of getting away from danger. Then it happened: the horrible sound of bodies falling through the brush. The cracking of tree limbs and moans from horse and human continued down the side of the steep canyon. The instant the first branch broke, Christy flew off my back. She knew there was trouble and didn't even wait until I came to a stop to dismount. She started calling Jim's name as she ran back down the trail. With all the twists and turns, I soon lost sight of her. I turned around and froze in my tracks. Panic was filling the air. Christy quickly organized the other riders and had them move up the trail to a clearing ahead.

Then she asked her friend, Lynn, to help gather all the lead ropes the riders had with them. They were hoping that when all the ropes were tied together, they would be long enough to reach the fallen horse and rider. When one of the riders came to move me up the trail, I refused to move. No matter how hard she tugged on my bridle, I would not leave the spot where my precious rider had jumped off my back. Until I could see her face and hear a calmness in her voice, I was not leaving that spot. The rider gave up on me and continued to move the other horses. I slowly moved down the trail just far enough to see around the corner to where Christy and Lynn were working. They were trying to break branches with their bare hands and open a path down the side of the cliff. All the time, Christy was calling Jim's name and kept him engaged in conversation to keep him alert while assessing his injuries. He was disoriented but conscious. Christy and Lynn asked another man who was riding with the group to assist in helping them pull on the ropes. Christy finally climbed down the side of the canyon close enough to hand the end of the lead ropes to Jim. She then told him to take his saddle off his horse and they pulled it back up through the path of broken branches that they had made. Lynn was strong enough to break the tough manzanita and she kept working at enlarging the path. When Christy got back to Jim again with the ropes, she told him to attach the line to his horse's halter, turn the horse's head in the direction of the path, get behind his horse, and push. The horse was starting to go into shock and was not completely focused on getting out of the canyon. Jim said there were no major injuries on either of them but they were having trouble getting the horse to climb out over the brush. Jim picked up a broken branch and started tapping his horse on the rump. The horse finally lunged forward, hooves striking the air and madly throwing his legs in every direction. Christy and her helpers pulled and pulled to keep the horse moving forward. Eventually, exhausted and head hanging low, the horse was standing once again on the trail. Quickly, Christy climbed back down through the brush and had Jim wrap the ropes around his waist and the pulling began again. Jim was pulled to safety.

The miraculous outcome of this terrifying accident was that horse and rider had no major injuries, just cuts, puncture wounds, scrapes, and even a cracked helmet. There was still some distance remaining to camp, but everyone took it slow. Some riders even led their horses as they were too upset to ride. When Christy was through getting everyone underway, she turned her attention to me. She asked one rider why I had not been taken to the clearing. She was told that no force would budge me and of my faithfulness and devotion not to leave that spot. She walked up to me and hugged my neck with a stronger grip than she had ever used before. I felt moisture under my mane and her whole body was trembling. She was trying very hard not to cry out loud. I think it was a big release that the horror was all over. This time it was I who comforted her.

THE TWILIGHT YEARS

Twilight years. I was deep in thought as to the meaning of those words. A visitor to the ranch, a man whose face resembled well-worn leather, said those words when Christy told him my age. Thirty was just a number to me, and twilight, well, it was a time in the day just before dark. I was still vibrant and living my dream. I had a smile in my heart for every mile Christy and I traveled together. I was full of pride for all the hundreds of people I taught to ride. I was thinking it was me that introduced the first passionate feelings to men, women, boys, and girls about horses. Nothing has changed about me, so I wonder why humans think I should act any different just because I am thirty?

Christy was busier these days judging horse shows; campaigning her re-trained race horse, Smoke; and enjoying the versatile classes she and Smoke were winning in the English divisions. We stopped chasing cows for awhile, and I found that I enjoyed the longer rest periods between lessons and trail rides. Then little Suzie showed up. She was a tiny, thin girl of nine years. She had begged her mom for riding lessons. Many parents hope that their children will eventually get tired of the routine, the chores, and the dirt and sweat that go along with caring for us during a riding lesson, but then there are those who discover they can't get enough of horses. Little Suzie was like a sponge. She spent long hours here at the stable. She loved cleaning my hooves and she started bagging my tail so it would grow longer. She had to use a ladder to put the smaller kid's western saddle on my back. She didn't have to use the ladder to put my bridle on; I willingly dropped my head for her. When she mastered the western style of riding, she progressed to hunt seat. But that wasn't the end of it. She wanted to jump. Now this could be fun, I thought.

Christy took it slow, teaching Suzie how to ride ground poles and lope overs. Timing and distance were the foundation of jumping so my rider would be safe and have fun, too. We used a lot of cross-bar jumps to help Suzie focus on the center of the jump. But she got a little sloppy with her turns and would not get me lined up in time for me to make a good approach. It was time for me to teach her that it would not be a good or safe jump that way. If she guided me to far off center, I would just stop and not jump. She learned quickly to tighten her seat as well, as she ate dirt a few times for lunch! If she brought me in to far at an angle that put me parallel with the jump, I would just stop again. But I guess the old Roger Dodger was still in me, because I could pivot around, and take the jump from a standstill. I think my training methods worked well as they made Suzie pay attention. Soon Christy suggested to Suzie's mom that Suzie was ready for her first small schooling show. My strength, experience, and stability made me the perfect mount for Suzie's first ride in the show arena. Boy, was I pampered the day before the show. Suzie clipped my whiskers, bridle path, and chin hairs. I was given a complete bath with sweet- smelling girly shampoo and my tail was deep-conditioned. I was put on the hot walker and dried as Suzie cleaned the saddle and bridle. The trailer was loaded with fresh shavings for me to stand on, and my breakfast was placed in the feeder so I could munch on the way to the show grounds the next day. Finally, I was wrapped up in a hood to cover my head and mane, and a blanket that would keep me warm and clean all through the night. I was put in a stall next to the champion ladies of the ranch, Pretty Pie and Smoke. A ranch horse never had it so good! I slept well that night.

I was in a deep sleep when the barn lights came on. I heard, "Ranger, it's time to go." Christy put my halter on and led me to the trailer where she wrapped my legs for protection. I was told that we would meet Suzie and her mom at the show grounds. I hopped into my matching truck and trailer and started to enjoy the hay prepared for me.

The show grounds were buzzing with excitement, and so was I as this was my first horse show of this type. There were all sizes and colors of horses tied to trailers or being lunged in the warm-up arena. A few whinnies filled the air, coming from horses that were nervous about being away from their stable-mates. Human friends were greeting each other and trainers were barking instructions to students who seemed less prepared than little Suzie. I was given a drink of water, saddled, and groomed with some hair polish. I was stylin'! Christy entered Suzie in cross-bar hunters; a class that looked like our practice jumps. They lead me up to the arena fence and we all studied the course together. Eight fences seemed like a lot for a nine-year-old girl to remember. I was ready to help her if she started to lose her way. I'll just suggest with the turn of my head, I thought, just like I did with Jim in the mountains long ago. Then Christy gave Suzie her standard advice she gave to all her students before entering an arena, "It's okay to have butterflies," she said, "just as long as they fly in formation!" The announcer called Suzie's number and we entered the arena. I was so excited to be doing this, but sensed tension in Suzie. I think she stopped breathing. I knew a way to calm my riders down and let them know everything was alright. I took a deep breath and gave out a nostril sound - horsey yoga. It worked. Little Suzie followed my lead and did the same thing. She took a deep breath and let it out slowly. We proceeded on course. She learned her lessons well and we kept a good pace, meeting each jump in the center. An outside line, two fences, a diagonal line, two fences, another outside line, two fences, and the final line toward the gate, two more fences. We did it! Little Suzie guided me well and when we finished the last fence, she remembered to trot a circle with me so the judge could see that I was still sound and a happy working hunter. All our family and friends came running to us when we left the arena. I lost count of how many hugs I got in just those few minutes. It took some time for all the riders to take their turns in the class, but finally the results were in from the judges' card. My ears perked up when I heard my name mentioned. We took third place! Suzie and Christy were so happy, that it was like first place to them. The class was big with 23 entries. It was quite an accomplishment for a little nine-year-old girl and a little thirty-year-old horse. Twilight? I don't think so. More like the dawn arising!

A RIDE WITH PRIDE

Fall was approaching. The leaves on the trees that shaded me all summer were now a colorful display of orange and yellow. Just as the trees needed a rest from their growing season, I sensed that it was my fall and a resting time in my life. I was a little slower in my recovery when I ran or jumped. My muscles were not as defined as when I was a colt. I was content with fewer lessons and trail rides, and Christy made sure I did not have to carry anyone that was too heavy.

During the first week of October, Christy and Steve were invited to ride with a private riding club from Southern California. Plans were made to go, but a wild fire broke out in Northern California and Steve was assigned as the chief investigator for the fire. Christy called her riding friend, Lynn, and she filled in for Steve. Christy could have ridden any one of her younger horses in training or one of her finished show horses, but instead she chose me. She told Lynn that she wanted a steadfast, surefooted, and reliable mount that could go down the trail on its own. She wanted to be able to relax and visit with the other riders. I would do that for her so she could get to know all the people. Lynn rode a paint filly that was in training at the ranch.

The filly and I were loaded into Christy's truck and trailer and driven five hours to a secluded mountain property. The road in was sandy and went through several canyons. It was like an outlaw hideout. Upon our arrival, I found all the comforts of home were there waiting for us in this camp. I had my own pipe corral with an oak tree for shade growing alongside and all the quality alfalfa hay I could eat. The people were friendly and welcomed us. As I carried Christy down the trail, the riders talked about how the group got started. About eighty years ago, when the West was being settled, ranches were large and spread out over hundreds of acres. When the time came to gather the cattle from the range and mountains, ranchers would ride to their neighbors' ranches and all pitch in to get the job done. Then every rider would move from ranch to ranch until the work was finished. I just knew that some of those early ranch horses were my ancestors. I could see myself doing that kind of work. That was the same adventurous spirit I had inside of me. As I looked at all the other horses on the ride that weekend, I wondered if they took pride in the history in which they were participating. I surely did. At thirty-one I was living history on the hoof as well.

There were several water breaks for horses and refreshment breaks for the riders. As all the riders made their way into a clearing that was used for large groups, wagons pulled in from behind us. I had seen a single horse pulling a cart at our ranch when Christy was training him for the show arena, but never anything like this before. These wagons drove right out of the history books. There were four up and six up, meaning the number of horses that were hitched to the wagon. The wheels were large and had wooden spokes. The horses wore heavy collars and when they walked, the large chains that attached the double-tree to the wagons clanged like bells. It was a sound out of the Old West. I think I worried Christy a little as my head went up and my eyes opened wide to take it all in. It wasn't fear, just pure enjoyment.

That night as I munched on my hay, content in my own little corral, I watched how the humans celebrated being a part of the Old West. They were dressed in fringed jackets, vests, high-top cowboy boots, Western hats, scarves, and blue jeans. There was a music band playing old Western songs. A Western barn, much like the one I lived in at home, was open on three sides with a longhorn lamp hanging from the center beam. Sawdust and shavings covered a dirt floor and old whiskey barrels were used for trash cans. I watched Christy and Lynn sit around a huge campfire visiting with people. Christy never stopped smiling. Later, I heard Christy and Lynn comment that the food was like being on an ocean cruise, only on horseback. I am glad that Christy and I got to share this "first" together. It would be a lifetime association for her and Steve.

IT'S TIME TO GO

I turned thirty-two this year. That must be a record in horse years. I wonder if there is an award for that, but then that is easy to answer. Just look at my life. It's full of rewards. I wish all horses could be as happy as I am. I think I look pretty fit for my age. My tail now drags the ground, thanks to it being kept in a bag all these years. And I actually have some white hairs showing up on my hips and flanks with a speckle or two of mottled skin. Is it possible I am turning into an Appaloosa or is it just wishful thinking? Living with the spotted breed may have rubbed off on me, and no one really had any idea of my mother's and father's backgrounds, so who knows?

These days I am feeling a few twinges and small sharp, pains in my sides from time to time. I can't figure it out. I don't gobble my food or drink too much at one time. I do feel the need to stretch extra long when I try to urinate and then sometimes it takes a while for anything to come out. I still have a good appetite. I don't want to worry Christy, so I will try not to show her that I am in any discomfort.

Our annual coast ride was moved to September this year because Christy was out of the country judging in June. Another black and white colt was born at the ranch last spring and Christy wanted him to get his "Ranger experience" at the beach. I am always honored and take pride in my responsibility of training of the young colts. I know the coast trip will take my mind off of my side aches, and Christy and I will once again enjoy the trails and sand dunes together. This late in the year gave us an extra bonus of the monarch butterfly migration. The campground was covered in bright orange and black butterflies frolicking around the water trough. One of the riders walked through the middle of the flock just to see them scatter and fly away. As they flew upward, she noticed a sticker on the wing of one butterfly. She said it had a phone number on it. Everyone in camp thought she was crazy, but she yelled to get a pen and paper and write down what she repeated. Humans were scrambling to find something to write on as she called the number out. Later, they called the number and, sure enough, it was legitimate. It seems that government officials are tracking the migration and appreciate when people take the time to call in so the butterflies can be tracked on the distance they travel in a certain period of time. I studied the butterflies as they flew in all directions. I remember Christy talking to her students when they were nervous about a task they had to perform on horseback and getting butterflies in their tummies, "Just make them fly in formation," She said. She was wise in helping people find their joy in riding.

After the coast trip, I could have used a lift from those butterflies. I was spending more time lying down. My energy was lower than usual and Christy noticed right away. She had the veterinarian come for a visit. He drew some blood from me. The blood tests showed I had a kidney problem. So I was started on a blood builder that would give me a boost. It worked for awhile.

Four weeks passed and Christy and Steve were getting ready to head for their annual club ride in Southern California. Christy came to my paddock a few days before she left and said, "Sorry Ranger, old buddy, but I think rest is the prescription for you at this time." Her voice was shaky and I sensed concern in her words. Am I really that sick, I thought? I'm not ready to end this life; I need a few more rides with my little lady. I had a favorite spot in my paddock that I liked to stand. It was on top of a small hill, just high enough to give me a better view of the mountains and the upper river canyon that I loved so much. Christy brought in a few bales of shavings and spread them there for me. She wanted me to be comfortable while she was away. Despair filled my heart as I watched her pull out of the driveway Friday morning without me in the trailer. I must hold on to see her one last time, I thought with earnest. Then I lay down to ease the pain in my side.

I struggled all weekend to function as a normal horse. But just the walk to the water tub became a chore. I tried real hard to focus on my life at the ranch and the people I loved so much. As I lay in my bed of shavings, I thanked the Great Creator for allowing me to live among the hills, canyons, oaks, streams and rivers, to smell fresh cut grass, eat luscious alfalfa and oats ,and hear dogs bark, birds sing, and cows moo. How blessed I have been to belong to Christy and Steve. I was wondering how much longer I could hold on, when Christy's dad came to the fence to check on me. He had taken care of me many times when Christy was out of town showing or judging. He knew instantly that I was not well. Lou took his cell phone out of his pocket and called the veterinarian.

Forty-five minutes later a horse doctor was at the ranch to examine me. His hands were kind and gentle. He kept repeating to me, "I'm sorry, old fella." After a through check, he instructed Lou to get me to the Vet clinic as soon as Christy returned from her Southern California ride. Then Lou had to make the hardest phone call of his life. He had to tell Christy I was dying. He was standing close enough to me that I heard the voice on the other end of the phone yell, "NO! Please tell Ranger to hold on for me, please, please." I knew it was Christy's voice. Steve and Christy had just broken camp and were already heading home, but the doctor did not think I would last as long as it would take them to make the drive home. He started an IV in my neck and hung the life-support bottle in a nearby oak tree. I knew he was helping me and I lay still in hopes the liquid he was dripping into me would help me continue this life long enough to grant Christy her wish. Lou made another phone call and an hour later a backhoe arrived. I knew what this was for. I had said goodbye to Tiger, and Kyappo my other horse friends in this same manner. I knew I wasn't really dying forever, as I was having thoughts about meeting my Creator. I had heard Christy talk about Heaven and how she hoped animals would be there. To her it was a beautiful place with eternal peace and joy. I was ready to go there and wait for her.

It was late in the afternoon when I heard the truck and trailer pull into the ranch driveway. Steve barely got the truck stopped before the door flew open and Christy hit the ground running. She had a paper in her hand. As she got closer to me, I saw her tear- stained face and red eyes. She collapsed onto the ground next to me. "Ranger, Ranger, my beloved Ranger," she cried. "I'm sorry you had to suffer by waiting for me, but I am glad to see you one more time." "I wrote you a letter while we were driving home," she continued with tears streaming down her face. She began to read it to me, holding the paper in one hand and stroking me softly with the other.

I am writing this to you, Ranger, as I contemplate the last few hours of your life. I am hours away from you, driving home from the club ride where you brought me such joy just a year ago as my mount. Please hold on, my friend, so I may hug and kiss you one more time. I pray you will be comfortable until I get there.

I have been the lucky one to have had you I my life. The Nelsons were happy to raise you as a young colt. Their whole family shared the experience of learning to ride from you.

Steve is grateful for all the pack trips you took him on in the high country. And for the deer you carried out for him. Dan thought you were the greatest trail horse he had ever ridden, even getting him back to camp after dark (despite the log you jumped and caught him by surprise!).

You were a blessing to have as a lesson horse. Hundreds of children from ages 4 to 84 were taught the love of horses from your back.

And, Ranger, do you remember Larry, Rick, Patty, and Roy, who all had disabilities that kept them struggling for a normal life? They became superhuman when they rode you.

You were wonderful to let us use you as an English horse as well. What a thrill it was to jump fences in the arena and cross-country with you.

I was proud to team pen and sort cattle with you. Us two little shorties could make the cut and take home the winnings from time to time. You even took me gathering cattle for real in the foothills above the ranch.

You were phenomenal in the mountains, through the trees, over rocks, and forging streams.

How magnificent you were as a"pony horse" to all the foals I raised. How patient and tolerant you were with those youngsters. You seemed to know they looked up to you for guidance. Oh, how they trusted you. And so did I!

But the greatest joy you gave me was at the beach. My dream was YOU – the waves and the dunes!! I thank you for that!!

And at 29 you took my Dad, 82, on a beautiful mountain ride, still safe and sure- footed. It was great day with my two special guys!

Ranger, THANK YOU, THANK YOU for just being you. There will be no other horse that could ever take your place in my heart.

At this final moment of being physically together, our two souls connected for eternity and no other words were needed. As I laid my head down for the last time, the fading sparkle in my eye was all for her…..

HEAVEN BOUND

I felt refreshed. I was overwhelmed with the desire to get up and start walking up the trail that was set before me. And I did so with ease. There was a newness in the air like it was a spring morning. There were some curves on the trail and they followed a stream that flowed alongside the path. Just up ahead, the image of a man with long hair was sitting on a boulder near a pool of water that was being filled by a waterfall. How peaceful everything was to me. Then the man smiled at me and greeted me with "Howdy Ranger." I knew Him, and yet had never met Him. He knew my thoughts without me uttering a whinny.

Well done, Ranger, he said. You took care of all the souls I sent your way. You were a noble steed and loved and served your owner well. I blessed you with a long life on Earth because you were doing everything so beautifully. Your spirit is one of my most precious creations. That was the whole point of your life. I wanted people to look past your outward appearance and to look at your heart. If they did this in all situations, then they would know the blessings of life that I would have for them.

I have a special place set aside for you. There you will find lush green grass, creeks flowing through your meadow, and willow trees shading your eternal home. And no fences! But, before you go there, I want you to know that even though Christy is broken- hearted at you leaving, she will love you for the rest of her natural life and someday she will join you here. She tearfully took a few of your tail hairs and had them braided onto a bridle that she uses on all her trail rides. She tells everyone that a part of you goes with her on every ride. She will be alright without you as I have sent her another horse to take care of her as you did. I have given her a beautiful bay mare she has named Dollar. They will have many adventures together. Dollar proudly wears your tail-hair bridle and looks forward to meeting you here someday. I am sure you two will have lots of Christy stories to share when you graze together in your beautiful meadow.

Now come with me, my champion war horse. You have a party to go to, Kyappo, Tiger, and Smoke are all waiting for you.............

CHRISTY WOOD

As a young girl, Christy dreamed of horses. The dream was to own that one special horse that would know her every thought and be her best friend. Christy had a few other horses before Ranger came along and she loved each one for their own special talents.

But when Christy met Ranger for the first time, their souls rejoiced and an instant bond developed that would last 30 years. The dream horse was soon purchased and the adventures began.

Christy's horse career has taken her across the United States and internationally as a multi-carded horse show judge. She has trained, ridden and won at World and National breed shows. Her first book, 'Your Best Horse Show, a guide for managers and exhibitors", has done well. But to stay grounded and find inner peace, Christy would saddle up Ranger and head out on the trails. Riding God's greatest creation, the horse, her Ranger, in the majestic mountains of Three Rivers, was the ultimate! She continues her trail riding enthusiasm by riding on the historic Chief Joseph Trail Ride, a thirteen hundred mile ride that takes thirteen years to complete. She and Dollar will earn their trail medallion award in 2013 for 10 consecutive rides together.

Christy can be reached at www.wdnhorse.com.

CPSIA information can be obtained
at www.ICGtesting.com
Printed in the USA
JSHW010029190123
36363JS00001B/7